MOUSE & LION

AESOP

RETOLD BY

RAND BURKERT

PICTURES BY

NANCY EKHOLM BURKERT

MICHAEL DI CAPUA BOOKS · SCHOLASTIC

MOUSE & LION

TEXT COPYRIGHT © 2011 BY RAND BURKERT

PICTURES COPYRIGHT © 2011 BY NANCY EKHOLM BURKERT

LIBRARY OF CONGRESS CONTROL NUMBER: 2010916970

PRINTED IN SINGAPORE   46

SCHOLASTIC, NEW YORK, NY 10012

TYPOGRAPHY BY KATHLEEN WESTRAY

FIRST EDITION, 2011

For Francesco and Roberto

RB & NEB

stay together

learn the flowers

go light

GARY SNYDER

ONE DAY, MOUSE, hurrying home, lost his way on a rocky ridge. He was in such a rush he scampered right over a tawny boulder that lay in his path.

Well, that boulder rolled
over and caught him by the tail.
It was King Lion, in a bad humor.

"Scampering over my back!
While I was asleep! I'm not going to
punish you, runt. I'm going to *eat* you!"

Mouse found barely
enough courage to squeak: "Sire,
I took you for a mountain—honestly!"

"Me, a mountain?" Lion mused. "That is possible."
He swung Mouse to his whiskery jaws and growled.

Mouse spun slowly as he dangled. He dangled as
he spun. He squinted into Lion's mouth, feeling
his warm breath, noting his yellowed teeth.

"Please let me go!" Mouse cried. "I promise
to be loyal! I'm a brave mouse, Sire.
Put me down and I'll show you."

"Brave indeed," said Lion. He did a lazy
half roll, and Mouse found himself back
on the ground. "Show me how brave you are!"

Mouse spied a tall blade of grass and hurled
himself at it, shouting, "WATCH ME!"

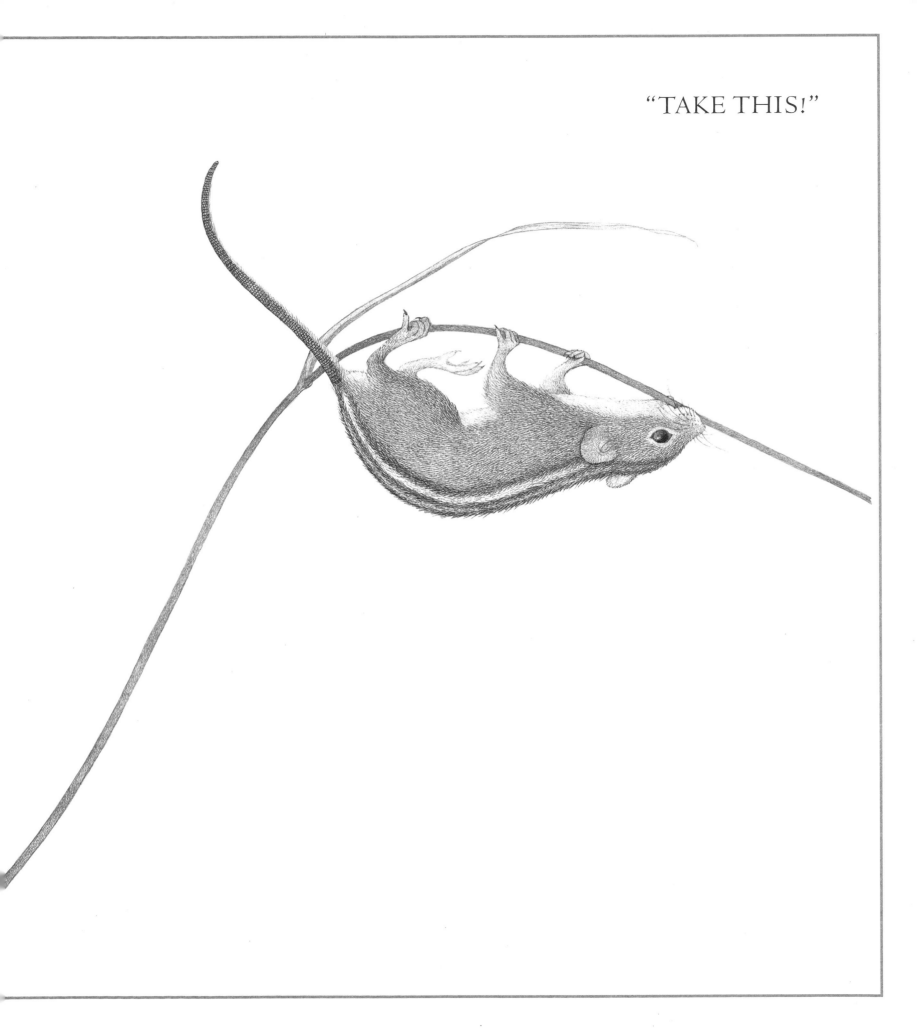

"TAKE THIS!"

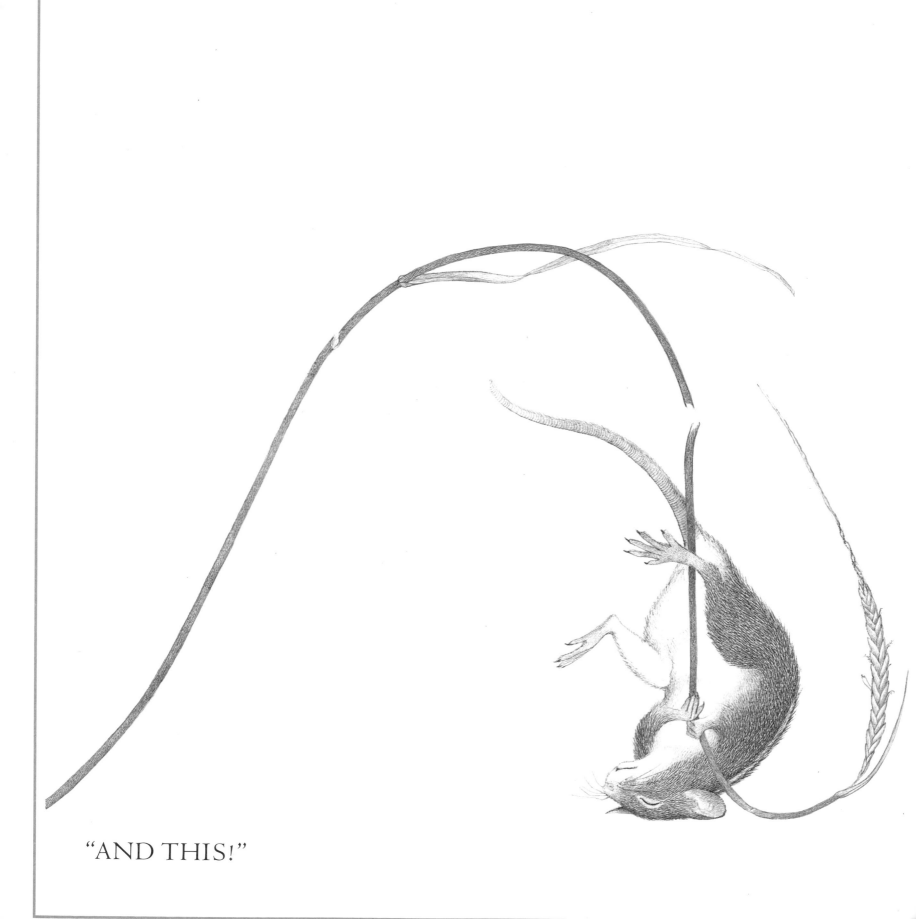

"AND THIS!"

"I see . . ." said Lion. "How many battles have you fought, little Mouse?"

"Believe me, King, I try to avoid them. I'm quite small, you see. But I don't avoid mountains. I go right over them if they're in my way.

"*Please* let me go!" Mouse begged. "You might need me someday, in a pinch."

Lion laughed and laughed. "*I* need *you*?
Good joke! But I like you, little Mouse. Go and
climb more mountains. And don't brag about your
bravery!" King Lion gave his paw to be kissed, but Mouse
meekly backed away. "Bless you, Sire—and goodbye!"

Mouse tripped over
his tail and rolled down the
ridge and out of sight. Lion
thought about him for a moment,
yawned, and soon fell back asleep.

A YEAR PASSED, and Lion forgot
all about his acquaintance. One
afternoon, a warm breeze in
the tall grass made him drowsy.

"Ah yes!" he thought. "A wink under
that old baobab tree—just the thing."
He padded into the leafy shade and
stumbled straight into a trap set by hunters.

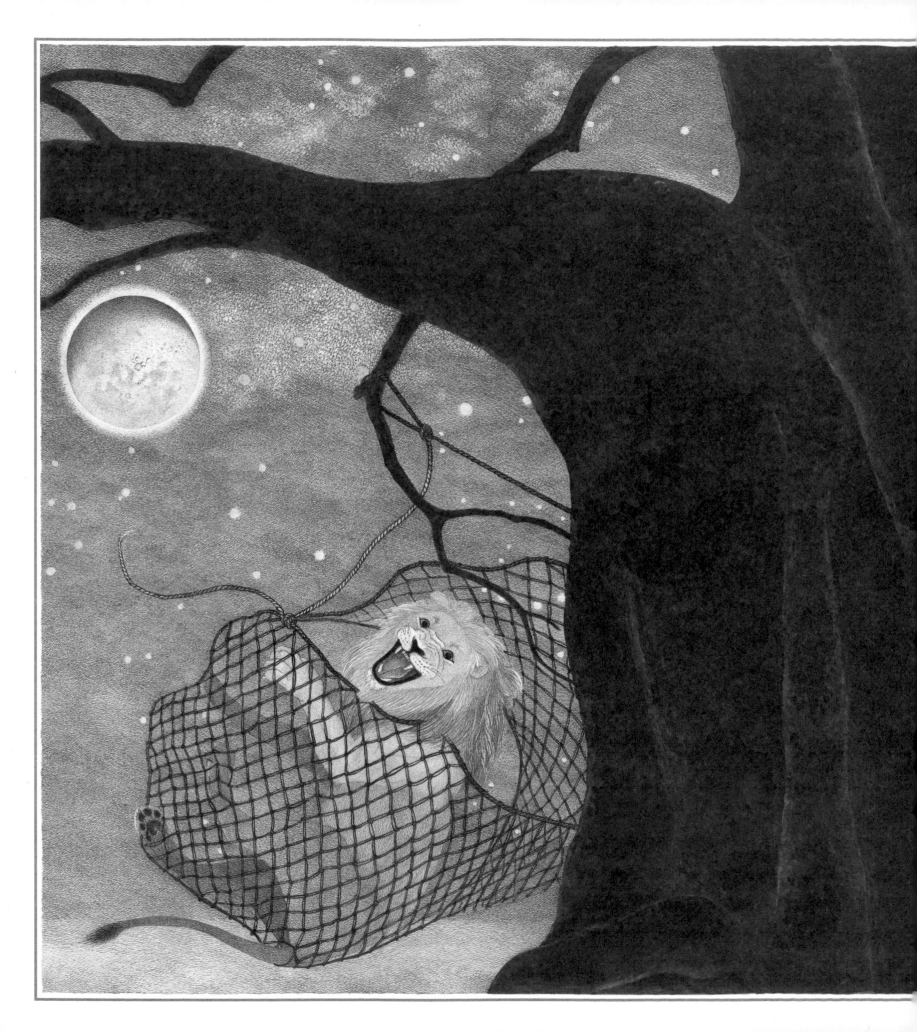

A net dropped and twisted around him!

The more he kicked and struggled, the more tightly it bound him. "It hurts!" he cried, but nobody heard him.

At sunrise, Mouse popped out
of his nest and sniffed.
He smelled Lion and
came running. "No
reason to be afraid of
our King," he said,
"no reason at all."

He found Lion
in a sorry tangle,
panting beneath
the baobab tree.
"O King," he said,
"do you remember
how you laughed at
me? I can help you now!"

"Little one," moaned
Lion, "what can you do?"

"Don't worry. My little
teeth are just what you need."

"You tell me not to worry!" Lion
grunted. "Good joke, little Mouse."

Mouse set to it, nibbling the net
and tickling Lion with his paws
as he scampered to and fro.

Finally Mouse declared,
"You are free, Lion —
Sire, I mean."

Lion stood up, shook his mane, and ROARED!

Then he crouched low to look in Mouse's eyes. Those little eyes seemed full of darting thoughts and things to do.

"You shall also be free, Mouse! I grant you liberty to climb every mountain in my kingdom. Even mountains that snore and rumble in their sleep, and roll over when you climb on them. Visit me again, my friend."

"I will," Mouse promised. "Now please—take care! Men are everywhere with traps to snare us, large and small."

LION WATCHED until Mouse
vanished between the rocks and grasses.

Then he, too, bounded away until he reached
the ridge, where he could stretch and dream
of bats
and beetles,
ants,
cicadas,
bright sunbirds,
and scampering mice.

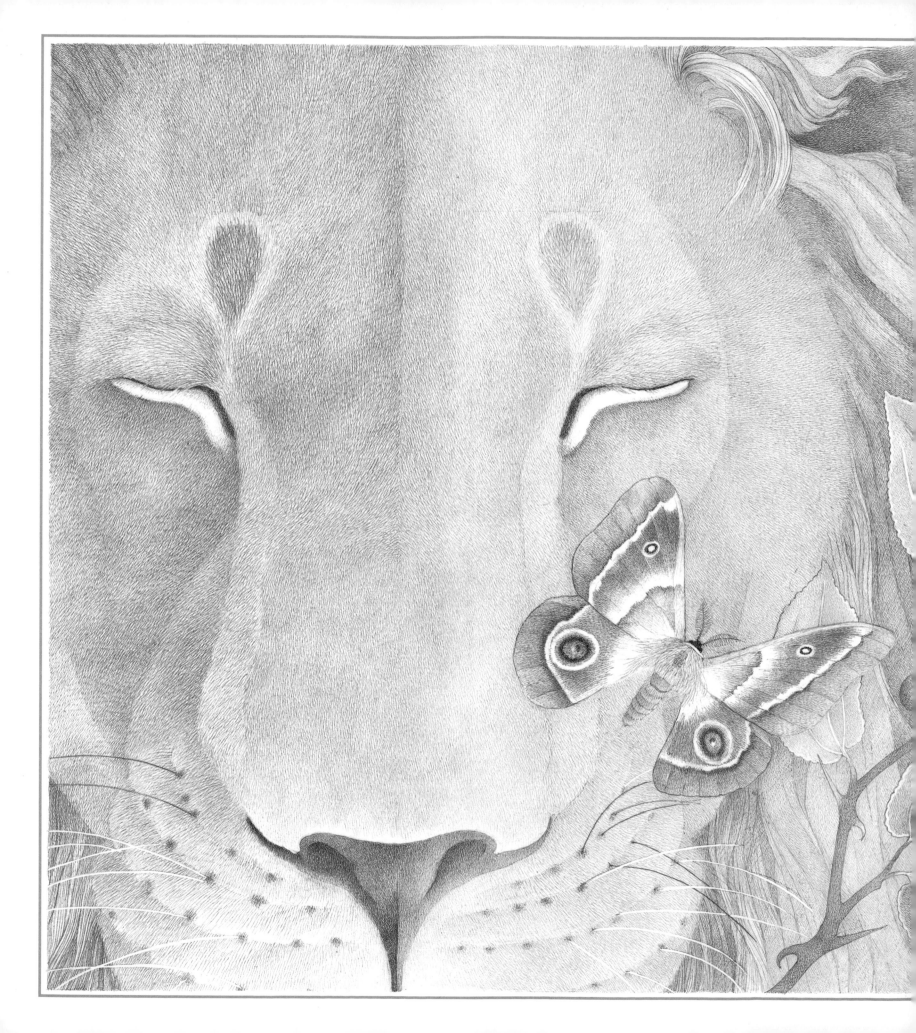

THAT DAY, SUCH SMALL THINGS MADE HIM HAPPY!

I N MOST PRODUCTIONS of this fable, Lion's name appears first on the marquee. It is not clear why this should be, when Mouse clearly performs the lion's share of the work. During the slow evolution of this book, Mouse's traits—busybody good will, keen teeth, streaming black/ochre coloration—earned him the deep affection of all involved. He receives top billing here.

In Nature—we know—lions enjoy a position at the top of a food pyramid. They nap, wake to eat, yawn, cavort, survey their realms and roar, then nap again. We may wonder: *When* are they truly worthy of their assigned role as King of Beasts?

Aesop—whether the Samian freed slave known to Aristotle or an apocryphal figure, part sophist, part African griot—proffered multiple views of Lion, clearly his favorite "character." In one fable, Lion agrees to go hunting with Fox and Ass, but when Ass insists on dividing the spoils equally, Lion devours him behind a tree. (He then asks Fox to split the meat, and Fox obligingly gives Lion everything, except for a bit of gristle. Lion asks: "Where did you learn to divide so well, Fox?" Fox replies: "From the Ass, naturally.") Yet in another fable, Lion maintains peace among all animals, and a gratified Hare sighs: "Oh, how I have longed to see this day, in which the weak shall take their place with impunity by the side of the strong." In *Mouse & Lion*, we catch the king at a midpoint between two poles, asleep to the true depth of his calling, not fully a despot, not fully a king.

We thank Aesop, whoever he may have been. He is, after all, a composite of many of our responsible ancestors, those who knew and preserved Animal Wisdom. And we thank the indigenous peoples who have never lost it.

Rand Burkert

. . . the hovering closeness of the world of myth to the actual world. / *Robert N. Bellah*

I N 2007, RAND completed his retellings of sixteen Aesop fables, with songs for guitar and voice to accompany them. In 2008, we began our collaboration on *Mouse & Lion*. Africa would be our "location," and I wanted to locate a place where an African mouse, baobab trees, and lions could be found together.

A region called the Succulent Karoo caught my attention, as did the studies by Professor Carsten Schradin of the four-striped African grass mouse, *Rhabdomys pumilio*. This is a diurnal, communally nesting, "basking" and "huddling" mouse, a lone forager, paternal in sharing the care of the young. But lions and baobabs do not exist in the Karoo. Dr. Schradin led me to Estelle Oosthuysen of Nhoma Camp in Namibia, who suggested that, in a relatively unexplored area bordering Botswana and Namibia called the Aha Hills, baobabs and lions might also be present. And so this story is set in the mysterious Aha Hills of my imagination.

Indigenous peoples have existed in this region for millennia. They are called San, or Bushmen, among them the Ju/'hoansi (!Kung). I am in awe of their supreme knowledge of plants and animals; of their music and dance as vehicles of healing and transcendence; of their equal sharing of all resources; and of their resilience even now in their plight of displacement from their ancestral lands. I thought this environment and culture a nourishing matrix for our *Mouse & Lion*.

Blue was in my mind, to conjure the "all-at-once" time, the "Everywhen" where past, present, and future coexist. Spirit and Light are continuous as my small brush and watercolors touch the white light of the paper.

I was enchanted to observe the little colony of *Rhabdomys pumilio* tenderly cared for in the Mouse House at the Bronx Zoo in New York. May these small creatures thrive as they forage for seeds and berries in the wilds of Africa, and may the great Kalahari lions survive to observe them kindly.

IN APPRECIATION

Dr. Carsten Schradin, Succulent Karoo Research Station, Goegap Nature Reserve, South Africa / Dr. Jeremy Burgess, freelance ecologist, Botswana / Dr. Paul F. Hoffman, Sturgis Hooper Professor of Geology, Emeritus, Harvard / David Aguilar, artist, Director of Public Affairs, Harvard-Smithsonian Center for Astrophysics / American Museum of Natural History / Snow Library, Orleans, MA / Aubrey Groskopf, Carol Phelon, Dr. Suzanne Anderson, Nigel Dennis, Chris Johns, *National Geographic* / *Kalahari Hunter-Gatherers*, edited by Richard B. Lee and Irven DeVore

Nancy Ekholm Burkert

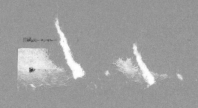